Swapna Haddow

WHY NOT?

The *almost* true story of stuff that actually happened in a library

Illustrated by

Daron Parton

SCHOLASTIC
SYDNEY AUCKLAND NEW YORK TORONTO LONDON MEXICO CITY
NEW DELHI HONG KONG BUENOS AIRES PUERTO RICO

For Team Scholastic NZ - thank you for everything ~ SH

To all the library-hibernating bears ~ DP

First published in 2025 by Scholastic New Zealand Limited
Private Bag 94407, Botany, Auckland 2163, New Zealand

Scholastic Australia Pty Limited
PO Box 579, Gosford, NSW 2250, Australia

ISBN 978-1-77543-917-2

A catalogue record for this book is available from the National Library of New Zealand.

12 11 10 9 8 7 6 5 4 3 2 1 5 6 7 8 9/2

Illustrations created using Adobe Photoshop and mixed media

Publishing team: Lynette Evans, Penny Scown and Abby Haverkamp
Designer: Vida Kelly
Typeset in Arima Madurai
Printed in China by RR Donnelley

Scholastic New Zealand's policy is to use papers that are renewable and made efficiently from wood grown in responsibly managed forests, so as to minimise its environmental footprint.

"SHH," Mum said, "I need to do some work while we're in the library. How about you go find a book to read . . .

and stay out of trouble!"

"I wouldn't climb up those shelves if I were you," the librarian said.

“Why not?”

"There's a family of hawks living up there
and I'm pretty sure it's almost time . . .

for their lunch."

"I wouldn't peel up that carpet if I were you," the librarian said.

Tomato
olives
GARDENING FOR CHILDREN
SHRUBS & HERBS
GARDENING

“Why not?”

"A bear came in last week and buried his half-eaten sandwich down there – and I'm not sure he'll be pleased to see someone digging it up."

Atlantic Oc
SHELLS
SEA
Oceans
Trees Vol 1
Trees Vol 2
TREES
Countryside.
Fishing

"I wouldn't take that book if I were you,"
the librarian said.

"Why not?"

"That's on hold for a pirate. His name is
Captain Don't-mess-wiv-me-books Blackbeard.
He loves reading and he's been waiting a long time for that one to be returned – and now it's back, he won't be happy to find that you've taken it," the librarian said.

“The last person to mess with old Blackbeard
was taken aboard his scurvy ship,
made to wash the deck and drink rotten
sardine juice out of a tin.”

"So you're telling me that the terrifying pirate

Captain Don't-mess-wiv-me-books Blackbeard

reads books about unicorns?"

"He does. And he loves unicorns," the librarian said.

“It seems pretty dangerous in a library.”

“It can be if you try to
climb the shelves,
peel up the carpet
or take a pirate’s book,”
the librarian said.

"I don't believe you.

I don't think there has ever been a hawk . . .

or a bear . . . or a half-eaten sandwich in a library.

And everyone knows pirates can't read."

"What's this?"

"Well, you probably won't believe me if I say it's a snake . . .
a huge, child-swallowing anaconda,"
said the librarian.

“You mean a snake that will EAT ME if I tug on the end of it . . .

"like this?"

"Oh, I wouldn't do that if I were you . . ."
the librarian warned.

"Why not?"

"Because there's going to be . . .

“a very annoyed mum at the end of that wire!”

UH-OH!